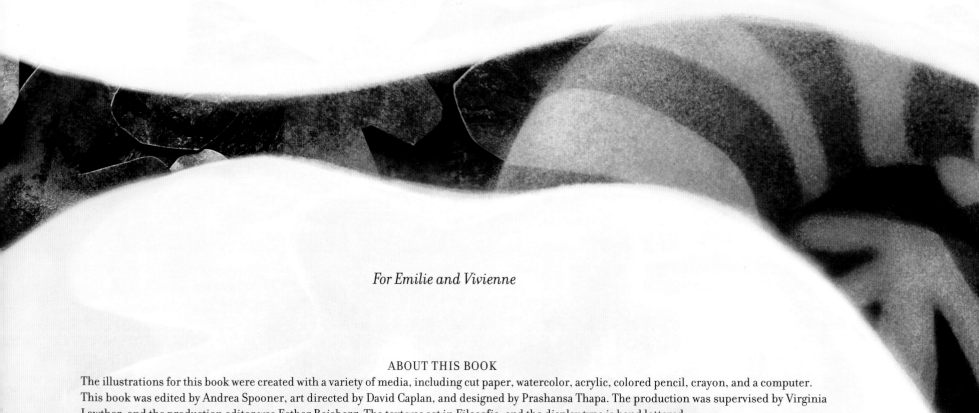

For Emilie and Vivienne

ABOUT THIS BOOK

The illustrations for this book were created with a variety of media, including cut paper, watercolor, acrylic, colored pencil, crayon, and a computer. This book was edited by Andrea Spooner, art directed by David Caplan, and designed by Prashansa Thapa. The production was supervised by Virginia Lawther, and the production editor was Esther Reisberg. The text was set in Filosofia, and the display type is hand lettered.

LITTLE, BROWN AND COMPANY

NEW YORK · BOSTON

Y DREAMING CREATURE

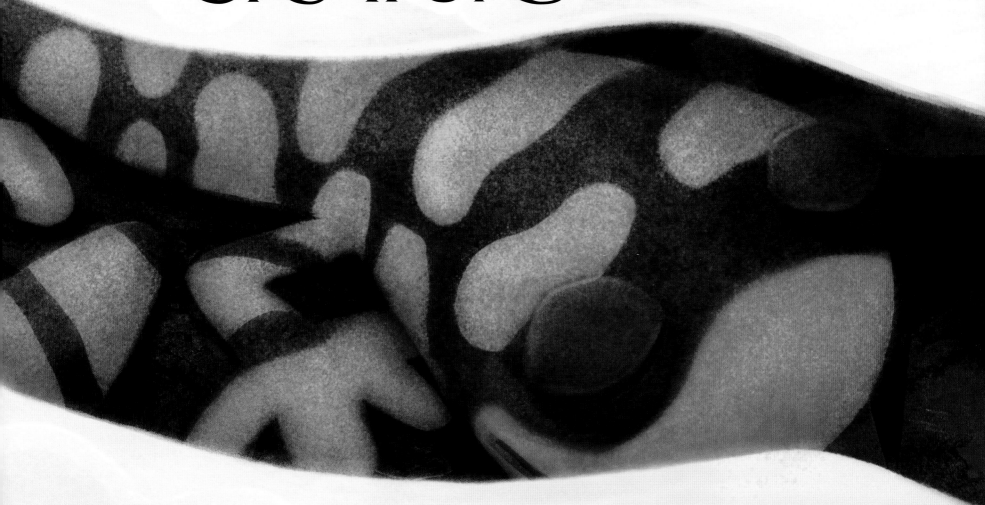

Brendan Wenzel

I had a dream I was a sleeping salamander.

All the world was safe, snug spaces and a warm, wet blanket of decaying leaves.

Secrets from the soil tickling my hands and soft belly.

A salamander . . .

until you came, with playful limbs, and woke me from that dream.

Then there I was. A drifting dancer, flowing freely.

All the world was curiosity, every new shape whirling, dancing with me.

Bursts of wonder tingling down the minds of my arms.

An octopus . . .

until you came, with calming waves, and woke me from that dream.

Then there I was. A graceful giant on a journey.

All the world was my swaying sisters and their stories, rumbling through the bulk of me.

Old paths pulling. Rain clouds singing, calling us on.

An elephant . . .

until you came, with your wild wind, and woke me from that dream.

Then there I was. A speeding pilot, soaring onward.

All the world stretched out below me, cool air whistling as it raced across my beak.

Feathers fluttering. Tucking. Rushing. Faster, faster!

A diving falcon . . .

until you came, with steady growls, and woke me from that dream.

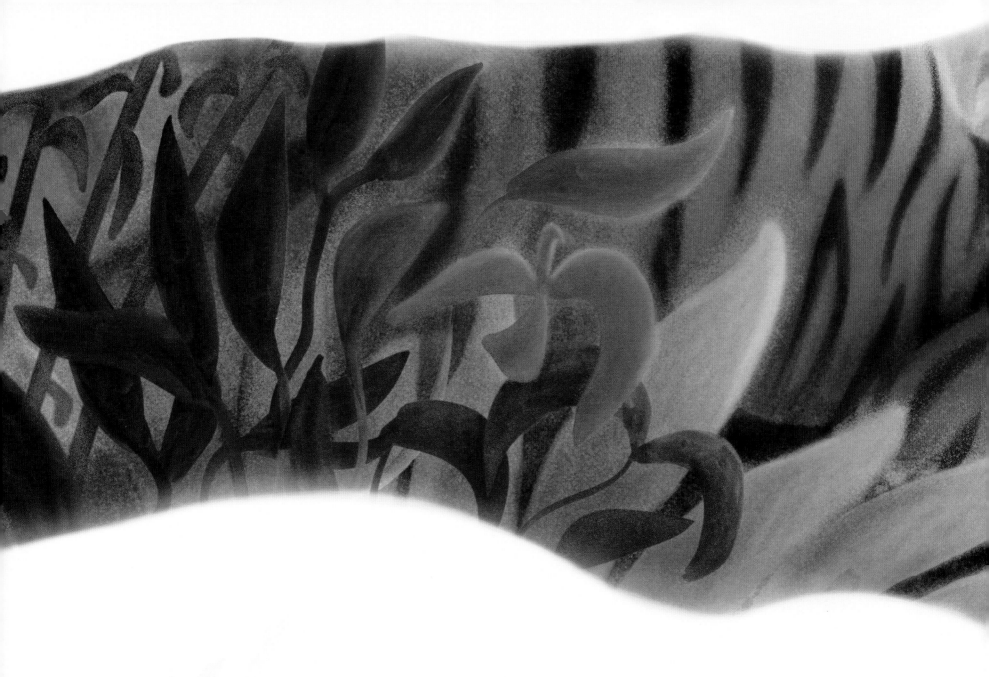

Then there I was. A silent hunter, sneaking slyly.

All the world was crackling dry twigs as I carefully placed my paw upon the earth.

Whiskers twitching. Sound in endless shimmering layers.

A prowling tiger . . .

until you came, with vibrant shades, and woke me from that dream.

Then there I was.
A bold performer, changing costumes.

Then there I was.
A brave explorer, burrowing below.

Then there I was.
A humming helper, seeking sweetness.

Then there I was.
A happy queen, returning home.

Then there I was.

Then there I was.

And was,

and was,

and was again.

In every dreaming creature,

sound asleep.

Until you came.

Then there I was.

A thumping heart and two waving hands.

All the world was play and wonder,

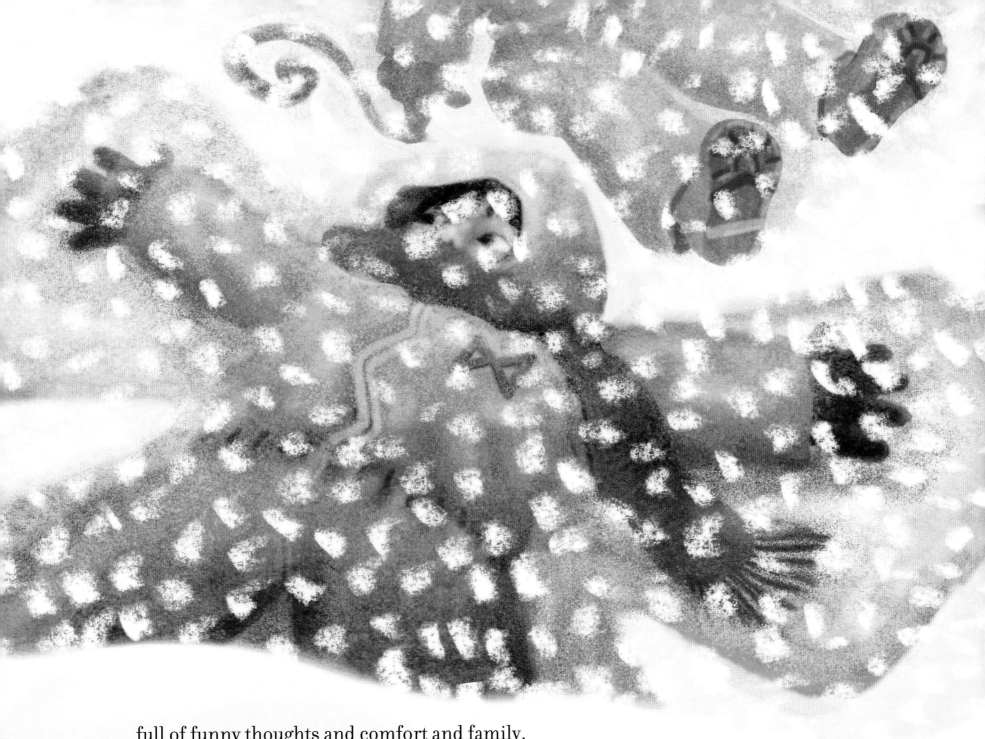

full of funny thoughts and comfort and family.

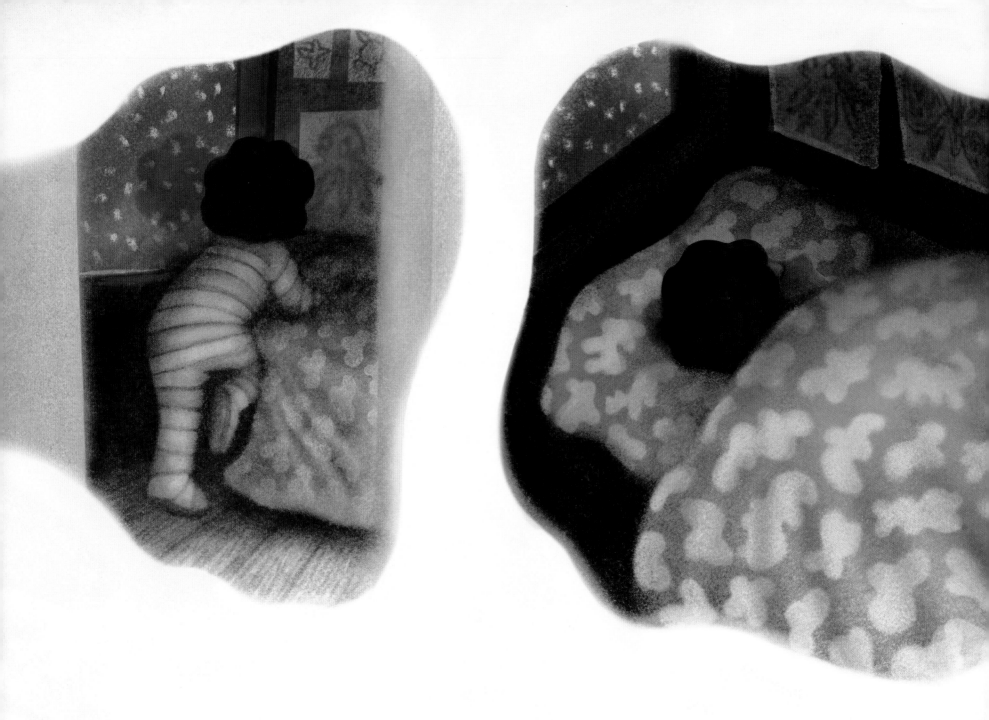

And as I slipped beneath the warm weight of a blanket,

I closed my wandering eyes and in that wild stillness . . .

. . . drifted toward a dream.